THE MYSTERIOUS ASSASIN

WARISHA

Copyright © Warisha
All Rights Reserved.

This book has been published with all efforts taken to make the material error-free after the consent of the author. However, the author and the publisher do not assume and hereby disclaim any liability to any party for any loss, damage, or disruption caused by errors or omissions, whether such errors or omissions result from negligence, accident, or any other cause.

While every effort has been made to avoid any mistake or omission, this publication is being sold on the condition and understanding that neither the author nor the publishers or printers would be liable in any manner to any person by reason of any mistake or omission in this publication or for any action taken or omitted to be taken or advice rendered or accepted on the basis of this work. For any defect in printing or binding the publishers will be liable only to replace the defective copy by another copy of this work then available.

Contents

Acknowledgements

My brother helped me a lot in writing this book,
When i had wrote this story and i showed to him he said
wow, what a mess you must add something more and
because of him i have rewrite my story and not only this
but he also helped me in choosing cover picture
and he is the one who has given this book title.

CHAPTER ONE

Once upon a time there was a happy family, Lium noah , Louella noah and their 8 month old son Both Husband and Wife loved his son so much, but one day a Strange person
entered home wearing Black Mask and an Old watch with 4 other Gang Members and Shooted both husband and wife, the Criminal was about to Shoot Lium's son, his
bestfriend entered , because of the panic one of them shooted their son as well. when Lium's best friend Arrived, he saw his friend died along with his wife and son,
but when he checked he notice that the criminal has shooted on the shoulder of their son, it wans't his heart, he rush into the hospital and called the police,
Police was unable to find the criminal, they were cluecless, this is the first case they are unable to solve.
the two Question remained a Question:
Who was the Assasin? And is Lium's son Alive?

CHAPTER TWO

It was a full Moon day the weather was clear and pleasant, the wind was blowing softly,shadow of the trees were looking beautiful, people were sleeping,

it was 2PM glowing night, streets were silent but there was just this one sound like someone is coming, ohhh yaaah its Zane lucus, a 14 years old high school boy who

often loves to skate on silent street at night.He was jumping with excitement, he knows amazing moves.Suddenly his alarm beeeped, it was time to go home

as he entered his father(lucus) was standing over there.

Lucus: Zane! be a little mature look at the time its 2:40AM, I was worried about you.

Zane: Dad you know I love skating, mostly at night.

Lucus: come on in have your dinner.

Zane: I'm not hungry dad, I have eaten chips and some sandwiches.

Lucus: Did you packed everything?, Tomorrow is your big Day.

Zane: (zane remained silent)

Lucus: What's wrong Zane, Aren't you happy?

Zane: Dad why are you sending me to the boarding school, I'm just 14 Dad, after Mother who is left it's you Dad. I can't live without you.

Lucus: I can't live without you too zane, but its not about togetherness, for me your life is important, and if (He will find me He will kill you too).

Zane: (confused)

Zane: who will find us, Dad what are you talking about?

Lucus: oh! umm! nothing, Look Zane boarding school isn't that bad

, you will make a lot of friends there and can sneak out of the hostel as well.

Zane: But you won't be there!

Lucus: No Zane I'll be always there for you, might not be physically but always emotionally, and you are my soul, Always remember Daddy is with you.

Zane: thanx Dad, you are the best.

Lucus: And when you will grow up you will get to know why I had send you to #boarding school.

Zane: Dad, I love you.

Lucus: Love you too , now have your dinner.

Zane: I don't wanna eat broccoli, can I have chips again I had put that in the kitchen drawer.

Lucus: I have two coke, shall we eat together?

Zane: Now we're talking. will you sleep with me today dad?

Lucus: okay, let's do this and how about watching your favourite movie with chips and coke.

Zane: Yipeee! this is the best night ever.

Now comeon Zane, lets play archery. hit in the middle, you are winning Zane. Dad, you missed your shoot, oh no!! Dad just one more chance and final decision.

OMG Zane you won, by the way your shots were amazing dad but you've lost the last one . yeah, are you happy my son,i know this is the least i can do for you.

no daddy this all means so much to me. okay, now sleep well and when you go to the boarding school make sure you work hard on studies and have fun, don't neglect

the fun part. Goodnight Zane, goodnight dad.

The next Morning Zane left his father's home and reached his Boarding school, He was very upset.

He wasn't able to find his room so he took help with

Senior boy and somehow he reached his room, Zane saw his roommate and said hi! his roommate said hi without even looking at him, he was busy in finding something and was very worried, he did't even looked at zane ,

zane sat on his bed and put everything in place ,whatever he had taken with him from his home ,till now his roommate was busy in finding something,

Suddenly He saw Zane,

Roommate: Wait, who are you? and how did you entered in my room ? are you a serial killer who goes in every hostel and kill boys?

Zane: Hey, Hey ,first lower your fry pan, are you gonna hit me with that!!

I've just said Hi and you have said Hi back to me.

Roommate: really i said .

Zane: yeah!

Roommate: oooh! im so sorry i was so busy in finding my Maggi, that didn't even rememeber that I've said hello to you.

Zane: That's okay,

so we are gonna live together.

Roommate: yeah! but I'm very sad, I had that last pack of maggie, I'll have to sneak out of the hostel for it again.

Zane: No you don't Have to.

Roommate: How, Do you have Magic or something?

Zane: No, I have total 10 piece of maggie, my dad had packed these for me.

Roommate: oooh!! thanx a lot, from now on you are my best friend

.

Zane: By the way, what's your Name ?

Roommate: oh sorry! im zion, zion mac.

Roommate: And what's your name?

Zane: I'm zane jasper.

Roommate: Wow, look at our names, zane and zion seems like brother isn't it, looks like we have a great future together.

Zane: what do you mean, are you gonna marry me ?

Zion: I'll see, If I won't find any girl, I'll surely marry you.

Zane: Is it raining ?

Zion: yeah, look outside the window, it looks so beautiful.

Zane: It indeed, so why your father send you in boarding school?

Zion: Well my parents were tired of my naughtiness, so they send me here to straighten me.

Zion: And why your parents has send you?

Zane: Not parents!, only dad.

Zion: Oh, im so sorry to hear that.

Zane: No it's okay, my dad send me here because, he is worrid about my life.

Zion: ohhhhhh okay.

Zion: okay zane its too late now ,I think we should sleep, we have class tomorrow, good night.

Zane: Good night.

Zane wasn't sleeping, He was just sitting on his bed and looking outside, it was still raining and the wind was blowing harsh and cold.

suddenly zion woke up because of the harsh wind,

Zion: hey, close that window.

Zane: oh! im sorry.

Zion: Are you a skateboard lover?

Zane: yeah! I love to skate, mostly at night, how do you know?

Zion: just by looking at your skateboard, i'm a skateboarder too, i sneak out of the hostel, I have broken many things and many times I have also been suspended.

all the teachers are tired of me. for fun, i break all the rules.

Zane: so, your status is very bad in hostel.

Zion: yeah, i must say with proud, that I'm the most evil student of this year.

I'm just letting you know about myself, whom you are getting into friendship.

Zane: I love evils.

Zane: So mr evil, shall we go outside for skating right now? in the rain, it will be so much fun, my father never let me did this, i always wanted to try this.

Zion: idea seems great to me, let's go partner, let me grab my skateboard and shoes.

Zane: And let me just change my T-shirt.

Zion: What's that mark on your shoulder?

Zane: oh! it's a bullet mark.

zion: Bullet mark?

Zane: yeah, when i was 8 months old, someone shooted me and i have this mark from then now.

Zion: it's Strange.

Zion: Whatever, let's go skating.

Zane: But where will we go?

Zion: Trust your partner, i always go there, and it's an amazing place for skating and relaxing , it's a silent street. And must wear your mask, so we don't get caught by that double chin.

Zane: double chin?

Zion: Yeah, the head of the captain of this entire hostle and headmistress'spoon.

And they both went to skate that night, first they enjoyed skating together then, they sat under the shadow of a big Tree:

Zane: you know what zion, i used to do this every night back at home but alone, this is the first time I'm with someone and it felt amazing to me.

Zion: you are right, having a friend like you is a blessing for me.

Zane: Are we gonna spend entire night over here?

Zion: What time is it?

Zane: it's 11:00PM.

Zion: oh shit!, this is the time when double chin gets active, and guard uncle will close the door, Hurry zane.

Zane: Oh no!

They were about to enter in the hostel, that double chin caught them red hand.

Headboy: Hello little dickens, Are you two coming from the party?

Zion: Your'e lying we went for skating.

Zane: woooow! zion, is he a double chin?

Zion: nonono! don't call him double chin on his face we say him on his back.

Zane: oops! um! hi, hi headboy.

Headboy: remove your masks?

Zion: don't remove it.

Headboy: Remove it, or you two wiil be send direct to the headmistress's office.

Zane: Headmistress'spoon.

Zion: You want me to be killed by this chubby? stay quite.

Headboy: What did you call me?

Zane: No, Nothing.

Headboy: You little evils, Directly to the headmistress office.

Zion: Get ready for another lecture.

Headboy: Miss they were disrespecting me, and they were out at this time 11:30.

Zion: lies again, it was 11:00 when we have entered in, it took 30 minutes of you to take us to the miss office.

Headmistress: who you two are?, remove your masks.

(they both removed their masks)

Headmistress: Zion, i knew it, and you new student are you his roommate?

Zane: Yes Miss.

Headmistress: Who am i kidding, doublechin I mean headboy make sure you change the room of zane.

Zane: No miss, it was my fault, I was the one who provoked him to go out for skating.

Headmistress: Whatever, you two are not living together.

Zane: But i want to live with Zion.

Headmistress: Enough, not a single word Zane.

Headmistress: Headboy show him his new room.

Headboy: Come along with me Zane.

Zion: I think Headmistress is right, if you will live with me you will be a complete failure because Honestly I'm a very bad student.

Zane: you're just a bad student not a bad boy.

Headboy: Hey stop talking , fetch out your stuff.

Zane: I'm gonna miss you.

Zion: Goodbye Zane!

Headboy: This is your new room.

Zane: Without roommate?

Headboy: yes, without roommate, haha enjoy.

Zane: I'm gonna teach you a lesson you double chin.

Headboy: Did you said something?

Zane: No, mind your own business.

Headboy: oh! I'm just dealing with my business ,I'm way more happier than ever, bah-bye,

the two friends torn apart, isn't it funny.

That night Zane didn't sleep all night he was thinking how to get back with Zion, on the other hand Zion was too so upset, he was awake all night.

when the two friends get up in the morning they saw headmistress was walking in panic.

Zane: Are you alright miss?

Headmistress: Zane look someone has just leaked out the maths paper of class 8. it's been just 35 secs, if director will get know he will fire me.

Zion: Oh no!

Headmistress: Zane, Do you know how do delete this account?

Zane: I'm Expert in this.

Headmistress: Oh! thankgod.

Zane: But on one condition?

Headmistress: what is it?

Zane: you will let me live with Zion.

Headmistree: okay, you two can live together, now do it fast.

Zane: just give me five miuntes, its done.

Headmistress: oh Zane! you are my saviour.

Zane: Thanx miss.

Zion: Wow! i never knew you're such a hero.

Zane: and an evil.

Zion: Evil?

Zane: I was the one who leaked the paper.

Zion: what?, why?

Zane: just to live with you, i knew that if i'll leak out the paper she can do anything for blocking that account, so i did it.

Zion: You did all these for me?

Zane: ofcoarse!

Zion: you're an Idiot.

Zane: ofcaorse I'm.

And lost friends get back together, but they were not done yet, headboy is their new target.

one evening when he was as usual walking in the hostel, Zane secretly went to his room and put sleeping pills in his bottle.

while he was asleep, Zane easily opened his cell phone by using his finger, and switched on his mobile internet.

(zane and zion were texting each other)

Zane: hey zion keep an eye on headboy.

Zion: leave it all to me partner.

Zane: so tell me buddy what should i do with him.

Zion: Can you hack his whatsapp?

Zane: It's my left hand job, partner.

Zion: alright! then do one thing hack his whatsapp and send him a fake text of headmistress that(headboy, I'm so sorry to announce you that you are no longer

a headboy of this hostel, and You are being suspended for a week because of your actions).

Zane: heeeeheeee! you've such an evil mind.

Zion: yup, I'm expert in these things, Zane we don't have much time do it fast.

Zane: just give me some minutes.

Zion: ok.

(after 10 minutes)

Zion: Are you done?

Zane: No, I'm having a little problem. just few more minutes.

Zion: ohno! he is about to wake up.

Zane: oh shit!

Zion: are you done?

Zane: just one more minute.

Zion: Zane, I'm dying in here.

Zane: done, you may leave his room, makesure to off his internet.
Zion: I've done that as i recieved your message.

after an hour when headboy wokeup, he opened his phone and saw something that he had never thought of, He was in panic (I'm being suspended because of my actions)
but what have i done.
He didn't get out of his room that evening and whenever he drinks that water he fall asleep.
on the other hand, Zion had announced to his classmates that headboy will not come downstairs today we can go out, in the evening all the students
almost 20 students were out at night, on the way back to their hostel headmistress saw all of them and called headboy.
when the phone rang double chin woke up and went to headmistress office.

Headmistress: I didn't expect you to be so careless.
Headboy: You suspended me for a week without any reason.
Headmistress: What?
Headboy: Look at this text.
Headmistress: And you believed in it without even asking to me.
Headboy: I thought it's true, but if you haven't texted me then who else?
Headmistress: Whoever has done that, i don't care, i've made you a headboy you should have ask to me.
Headboy: That's why i thought, why would you do that to me.
Headmistress: Headboy, you are really responsible but because of your carelessness Im actually suspending you for a week.
Headboy: But this isn't my fault.
Headmistress: ofcoarse it is, You believed on text without asking me and not only that but you also gave up your responsibility.
Headmistress: in this way anyone can make you fool and take advantage.
Headmistress: I'm sorry Headboy, you are being suspended for a week.
after one week you can rejoin your position.

Zane: It was important to teach him a lesson.
Zion: I fully support you partner.

They sneakout every night for skating, the hostel had one evil, but now they will have to deal with two.

CHAPTER THREE

Time passed, and that 14 years old Zane transformed into a handsome 17 years old young boy, But the things have changed Zane lives in an appartment without zion,

and zion lives with his parents.

Something happened to their friendship, the two friends were torn a part and the only reason for this was Zane's career, Zion many times tried to call but

Zane didn't picked up his call. He was so busy in his work that he completely forgotten his friend. He gives his time to his career and lefted skating.

The two friends were busy in their career, while growing up zane fall in love with business. He was busy in building his empire.

Somehow he launched his company but it didn't worked out, his company failed.

He got bankrupt two times but still didn't loose hope and put his all effort, he lost his health, he lost his happines, he lost his bestfriend, no party,

no outing, No proper diet he was just so busy in his career, career and career.

But all these paid off in his third attempt, company started getting profit.

on the other hand Zion too was building his business, he was in gadget business, he makes amazing AI based products.

but, his company was getting into loss.

Zane have an IT company he and his team build amazing websites, and softwares.

Zane's father(lucus) was very proud on him, But Zane wasn't happy even though his company was profitable, Zane was becoming rude, not to others but on himself.

He don't take rest, he either work or think about something.

It's been 3 years since both friends got separated. Zane is just living his life he never seems happy, his company employees were worried about him.

One evening when Zane was buying some fruits for himself in grocery, He saw someone and that guy was looking at him too, They both went closer to each other

and Zane suddenly recognised him:

Zane: Zion!

Zion: Zane!(they both hugged each others tightly Zane started crying)

Zane: Zion I'm really sorry for cutting you off for 3 years, I was never happy and will never be without you, Look at me what is my condition,

It's like I'm becoming a bad person every day, I was so depressed, everyday seems like I'm dying, I feel like there is no meaning in my life.

(Zion wipes Zane's tears)

Zion: And look at me, I'm not depressed nor it feels like I'm dying, but the only thing that i felt was I was no more happy without you.

Zane: Zion please forgive me!

Zion: Zane who am i to forgive you, I'm not even angry with you, but used to pray to the god that please get us back together,

and I'm so grateful to the god that he finally listened to me.

Zane: And i will never leave you again.

Zion: I love you Zane.

Zane: Love you too.

Zane: (zane told him by crying)so have you planned everything?

Zion: Huh! what plan?

Zane: about our wedding, but who will be wife, zion will you be my wife and i will be your husband after marriage.

Zion: stop it! haha, you still rememeber this.

Zane: how can i forget this.

Zane: Zion i wanna ask you a question?

Zion: And, what it is?

Zane: wanna eat maggie.

Zion: oh yeah! I'm still a maggie lover and shall we go for skating.

Zane: wow! i didn't even realised i've lefted skating completely.

Zion: let's do this, but not in this city, we are going to do skating where we have done it for the first time and got caught by that doublechin , Remember that?

Zane: How can i forget, let's go.

And the two friends were back, they both went to skate on that silent street.

Zane: This place is exactly the same.

Zion: yeah, nothing had changed.

After three years they both were doing skating, they were so happy and jumping like a 10 year old baby , hey Zane look at this move, i've learned it by myself,

wow that's really an amazing move, now look at me, this move i've just invented it, but it's not cooler than mine, yeah you're right, but i'm having sooo much fun

wohooooo!! watch out .

Zane: phew! that was a tiring stunt.

Zion: yeah! but we have a lots of fun, Zane I'm worrid about you, what happened to you?

Zane: after completing our hostel life my father send me to an appartment, completely alone, i used to play a lots of video games, but suddenly it struck in my mind

how games are build? i searched it on internet and it said, through coding. And that's how i fell in love with coding and business, but i didnn't even realised

that to achieve my goal i've lost everything, I'm just 20 but I don't have energy like a 20 year old, everyday feels meaningless to me I don't know why?

Zion: I know the reason.

Zion: Zane you cut me off but you also cut your father off, you didn't took care of your mental or physical health, you weren't connected with god,
the best piece of advice that i can give you is to have balance in life, try do balance everything in your life, do it and you will thank me.
well apart from all the reasons the biggest reason is staying away from me, you can't live happy without me darling, i complete you and you complete me
we are not friends we are brother.
Zane: we are brother, but how exactly i can balance everything.
Zion: it's very simple, just give everything your time, spend time with me, hangout with me, talk to your father, visit him everyday if not everyday makesure visit
him twice in a week, take care of your mental and physical health, maintain proper diet and have good sleep and give time to your business.
Zane: what will i do without you.
Zion: I'm never leaving you, only if you won't cut me off again.
Zane: I'll never ever , i promise you.

    And from that day they never cut each other off they were always together in each others highs and lows, zion taught him balance in life
and zane made his company profitable by investing money in it. they were struggling and grinding but they never left skating or hanging out together, zane visits
his father everyday. Zane's company employees were very happy to see change in him. after 5 years of complete hardwork he was invited by the most honourable
ceminar for awarding him as an young and creative entrepreneur of the year.
zion was very excited for zane, while zane was awarding, zion was cheering with excitement, they both went back home and right after one year zion was
awarded as an creative entrepreneur of the year , this time zane was cheering him up and was very excited for him, two friends are really

successful and happy
they are living their life in luxury after 9 years of grinding. They both had started their journey at the age of 17 now they are 25.

But the story haven't completed, Mystery yet to be solved.

CHAPTER FOUR

One day when Zane was as usual in his office working on his laptop, his manager came to him,

Manager: May I come in, sir.

Zane: Come in.

Manager: sorry for the interruption sir, dr.felix is here to see you.

Zane: okay, send him in.

Manager: okay sir.

Dr felix: Hi Zane, good to see you succeeding.

Zane: your company is also rocking.

Dr felix: Zane, where is your father?

Zane: why? you wanna meet him?

Dr felix: yeah.

Zane: you can tell me i will send him your message.

Dr felix: just leave it for now, When he will be back from his hometown makesure to inform me but not on call, bother to come to my office.

Zane: How did you know he is in his hometown?

Dr.felix: oh! um!, I'm getting late.

Dr felix: ok Zane, I should go.

Zane: ok, bye.

That night Zane and Zion were donating some foods and clothes to all the people who were old and helpless, they came across one such old house when they rang the
doorbell an old man came outside, The moment he saw Zane he was confused,

Oldman: Lium, Lium you're back(he started crying and hugged Zane, both the friends were confused).

Oldman: Lium my son, you were not dead.

Zane: I'm sorry sir, I'm not lium, I'm Zane lucus.

Oldman: Zane, Zane noah.

Zane: No, I'm Zane lucus.

Oldman: what's your father's full name?

Zane: Lucus, I don't even know his full name.

Oldman: Who is he?

Zane: He is Zion, my best friend.

Oldman: Zane show me your shoulder, do you have bullet mark?

Zion: yeah, he has.

Oldman: show me, exactly.

Oldman: Zane do you know how lium noah died.

Zane: who is lium noah?, and how his life story is conncted with me.

Oldman: Because you are a son of lium noah and louella noah, when you were just 8 months old they died, he killed them both, but lium's best friend lucus saved you.

Zion: And Zane you don't look like uncle lucus.

Zion: sir, whose pic is that?

Oldman: He is lium noah.

Zion: Zane, you look exactly like your father lium.

Zane: who are you?, and how do you know all these?

Oldman: I'm Mr. Robert, i was your's father's teacher, and his dad he calls me dad.

Zane: I'm confused, can you explain it to me deeply.

Zion: yes please explain it to us.

Mr. Robert: ok,

When your father lium was just 10 years old his mother i.e your Grandma died because of her kidney failure, he had a skateboard gifted by his mother, he loves to skate

mostly at night. After lium's mother death, your grandfather remarried a women and they both didn't liked lium, Lium used to do all the

household all throughout the days, at night he works on his project , after his mother death he had that passion to make medicines and vaccines for incurable diseases, and at a very young age he was expert in science.

I was his science teacher and a friend, he shares everything with me.

but one night when Lium was as usual working on his project his father i.e your grandfather came to him and said lium if you want to study you have to earn,

i can't afford your study,

your father was so innocent he had never disrespected his father, so he said ok father I wil earn.

that night lium called me and said i have to talk to you, When he told me everything,

I said i have one frined who needs a waiter and without any hesitation he joined as a waiter , after earning

his first wage he happily showed that to his father i.e to your grandfather, but your grandfather said give that money to me

and leave your study and work on another job,

if you want to live here.

Lium asked: but father I'm your son, at least give me a little time to be financial stable,

and then your grandfather said to your father either work somewhere else or leave my house,

your father asked to your grandfather: Don't you love me father?

what your grandfather replied: I had never loved you nor I will.

with a broken heart lium made a decision of leaving his home and came to me that night, I was surprised I thought he must be here for skating, but he started crying

and told me that i left my father's home, I said you are going to live with me.

he said no sir i can't, i have to go and he gone, I have to let him go, he left me with no

option. That night i was crying so that i can stop him, I was so afraid what if somethng happened to him, I asked him if you gonna fall ill who will look after you

he replied i will take care of my self, sir if you love me please let me go, and with a heavy heart I said goodbye to my son, for me he was no less than a son

and for him i was no less than a father, he calls me father. I made him do the promise that he will be in touch with me and he gone in that dark night it was raining.

after leaving, he was homeless for about 2 years no proper food, no proper dress, just working in a cafe and spend night under the tree, and sleepless night.

in the morning he works in the hotel and at night he works on his project.

after two years he was being made manager of that cafe, and from the last three years he was being approaching a famous scientist Dr. felix to be his assistant.

Zane: Dr felix?

Mr. Robert: Zane just listen, you will understand eveything.

and a year after your father bacame his assitant, and he was earning enough money so he hired a cook and that cook is your godfather (lucus), he is not your father.

lucus is with lium since then, They were very good friends, lium told all his secrets to lucus, and lucucs keeps that secret a secret.

after becoming an assitant, Dr. felix get to know that your father's experiments were much more better than him.

your father was a Manager as well as an Assistant of Dr. felix. After 2 years of being his assistant Lium learned a lot, so he started

his company of medicine and vaccine, but first it didn't worked, on his second chance, it started working out and his company was succeding

he left his assistant job and

a manager job, He was completely into business, his rule of the business was

earn and invest, but invest in two things 1. In other comapny or stocks, 2. invest it in charity, on poor people.

he always says, might the first investment cann't always be profitable but the second investment will never put you in loss, it will always pay back.

By looking him succeeding, Dr. felix approached him to take him in his company,
your father thought it's a grat option and he made him his company's chairperson and your father was the only Owner, CEO and founder of his company.
while working Dr. felix got an evil idea to spread diseases through these medicines, let me explain it to you two,
Dr Felix wanted to add some chemical in every medicines that can cure one disease but will leave another virus in the body
and he knew that lium will never let him do this, so he made a plan to eliminate lium and earn more money.
your father Lium didn't knew about his plan, but Lium had said to me once, that if anything happened to me plaese look after my son zane,
after achieveing success, Lium fall in love with a beautiful young lady louella.
One day when Lium was walking in the garden,
He saw a beutiful girl, she also saw Lium, they went closer and your mother had beautiful eyes, she drowned him in her eyes,
they fall in love with each other and got married,
they were true example of pure love, then they had you, but they gone, leaving you here.
that night you were ill, lium and louella both were with you, lucus was out for your medicine as soon as he entered
he saw guard died, lium and louella were dead, and someone had shooted you too but on your shoulder, and when lucus checked
your breathing you were alive, he rushed into hospital and called the police.
Lucus had recognised, it was dr felix
Lucus did't said anything to anyone beause He wanted you to be safe
Zane, lucus loved you like his own son he can even die for you.
lucus got married to a lady but she cheated on him, since then he never remarried and
He spent his life keeping you happy and safe, he was always away

from you

he send you to the boarding school just to keep you safe. because he knew that if Dr. felix will find him he will

not only kill him but also you.

your father Lium was very honest man and your mother was very innocent, they died too young Lium was 27 and louella was just 24.

Zane, your eyes are just like your mother's, and personality like your father's.

they loved you so much, you were their soul.

But they died.

Zane: Dr. felix, He is the killer of my parents?

Mr. Robert: Yes Zane.

Mr. Robert: lucus never told you, because you were not capable enough to raise your vioce against Dr.felix but now you have both political power and Money power.

Mr. Robert: The company "SPIRAL" is spreading virus.

Mr. Robert: You must stop him Zane.

Zane: I want to meet my father, Zion let's go and thankyou so much Mr. Robert.

will you come with me mr.robert?

Mr. Robert: ofcourse!

(Zane went to meet his father he hugged him tightly and thanked him for doing everything for him)

Lucus: where were you?

Zane: I was in Mr. Robert's house.

Lucus: So he told you the truth.

Zane: I understand why you were hiding all these from me.

Lucus: I was just waiting for the perfect time to come.

Mr.Robert: Lucus, so good to see you.

Lucus: Mr.Robert, thanx for telling him the truth.

Mr.Robert: He looks exactly like his father lium.

Lucus: Lium, my bestfriend!

Mr.Robert: Do you have any other secret of Lium.

Lucus: I have one more secret to tell, Zane bring your skateboard.

Zane: What's in it?

Lucus: It was your father's skateboard.

Zane: father!

Mr.Robert: It's too late now, Zane i think you should sleep.

Zion: yeah, zane come.

Zane: Can i stay here with you father just for one night.

Lucus: Zane, you should go to your home you look so tired, we will meet tomorrow.

Zane: okay.

Zane drove his car all the way to his home, He changed his clothes, hugged his pillow and started crying and imagining how painful it would be when he had shooted them.

I love you mom, dad and my dad (Lucus), I won't let you do this felix,

I was unaware but now, now you can't do anything, I will do and you will watch.

You want to kill my Dad (Lucus), I won't even let you touch him.

Zane: Zion, file the FIR report on Dr. felix.

Zion: What? are you out of your mind?

Zane: zion, I will first report FIR then only I'll go talk to him.

Zion: but he will be arrested

Zane: not wothout my permission, you just report FIR.

Zion: okay!

Zane: I'll go talk to him tomorrow.

Zion: I'm coming with you.

Zane: No, I'll go alone.

Zion: but why?

Zane: what if he shoot you?

Zion: so what, i'll die.

Zane: I can't loose you, bye.

Next morning Zane went to see Dr. felix and said police to stay outside, Zane had connected his mobile with police and whatever they both will say police can
hear them too.

Manager: (Excuse me sir, Mr.Zane is here to see you)

Dr.felix: (send him in)

Dr. felix: what brings you here zane?

Zane: I'm here to tell you that my father is back from his hometown, you wanted to meet him, right.

Dr. felix: oh ya ya, i want to meet him, will you be there with your father?

Zane: oh! I'm sorry i have some office work so i won't be there but make sure you come between 4-6PM in the evening because at night he is coming to visit me.

Zane: I'm getting late, bye.

Dr.felix: bye.

Zane was ready with police inside the home of his father, when felix arrived, his father meet him just like he used to, he welcomed him and said to sit down

after having conversation felix said, lucus did you know today is your last day? as soon as he started loading his gun to shoot lucus,

(Zane and police came in front of Dr Felix),

Zane: looks like you have your last day of your freedom.

Dr.felix: Zane Lucus!

Dr.felix: you've said you won't be here.

Zane: What did you think that you are the smartest and no one can be smarter than you,

You think I am so stupid, you are planning to kill my dad, I will not even know about it.

Zane: Now for the million dollar question, you killed my parents?

Dr.felix: you are Zane Noah.

Zane: Unfortunetly yes!

Dr.felix: I thought you were dead and lucus had adopted a boy.

Zane: you had shooted on my shoulder and my father i.e lucus saved me.

Dr.felix: Lucus I'm gonna kill you.

Zane: Don't you dare to touch him.

You were here to kill my father, right. Not to meet him but remember one thing, Zane is still alive.

In my life i won't let anything happen to my close ones, I have just three person My Dad, Mr. Robert and Zion,
even if you will look at them with your filthy eyes i will take your eyes off.
police, put him in jail.

Zane: Are you okay father?
Lucus: I'm so proud of you Zane.
Zane: I love you.
Lucus: love you too my son.

Having said that Zane recorded a video with the help of Zion in which he told all the truth about Dr.felix,
And refused people to use that company's product for sometime unless and untill all the products are toxic free.
He build team, recruited amazing scientists to make good and toxic free products and ordered to destroy all the toxic products so that no one can misuse it.
it took almost one year to completely replace toxic medicines into good and quality medicines.
It was hard for the consumer to trust that company again but Zane influence them and promised them quality product within one year company boomed
zane invest money what he earns from his fathers company into two things 1. he inhance the quality of the product 2. whatever left distribute all them into poor.
For 1 year zion was handling Zane's business and his own business.

Zane: thanx Zion, for looking after my business.
Zion: that was nothing.

Now Lucus and Zane is out of the danger, Zane was happy to do all these things and now he can look after his own business.
But the story doesn't end here,

One day when Zane was coming from his office he saw an old man shivering with cold, but the shops aroud there was close he couldn't buy anything,
he get out of his car and put on his jacket and muffler gave that old man some good amount of money.

He blessed him by saying, may god bless you with loving and caring partner and may god give you more money than you have.

After six months, Zane was walking on the silent street it was 2PM at night, winds were blowing soft and slow ,
he saw a girl sitting on the bench with her teddybear and talking to him.

Zane: would you mind if i sit here?

Girl: Yes Ofcoarse, sit down.

Zane: I heard you were talking with your teddy.

Girl: Sorry, sometimes I behave like a child.

Zane: You don't have friends?

Girl: How did you know?

Zane: I was just checking, You really don't have anyone.

Girl: No i Don't, I have this teddy.

Zane: you know what, you can try me out, I'm a good person.

Girl: I'll see.

Zane: Does this teddy speaks?

Girl: yeah, but only with me.

Zane: I'm really jealous with your teddy he is so close to you.

Girl: What do you mean?

Zane: Nothing, would you mind if i ask your name?

Girl: I'm Aayesha.

Zane: Aayesha Noah.

Girl: No, I'm just Aayesha i don't even know my full name.

Zane: Now you know, you are Aayesha noah.

Girl: What's your name?

Zane: I'm Zane noah.

After completing his business work, meeting with father and zion, he always come to that street because he always found her there, they spend time together and Zane get to know that Aayesha is so humble and nice girl he fell in love with her and she too, when Zane proposed to her She said yes, they got married and lived happily, after one year Zion got married too.

Now Zane has a life partner who is really caring and loving, Aayesha supports him in his lows and highs, Zane love her and respect her.

And there we go, if you invest on poor poeple it always pay back.

www.ingramcontent.com/pod-product-compliance
Lightning Source LLC
Chambersburg PA
CBHW071227140726
47996CB00004B/1517